Dear Parent:

Your child's love of reading starts here!

Every child learns to read in a different way and at his or her own speed. Some go back and forth between reading levels and read favorite books again and again. Others read through each level in order. You can help your young reader improve and become more confident by encouraging his or her own interests and abilities. From books your child reads with you to the first books he or she reads alone, there are I Can Read Books for every stage of reading:

SHARED READING
Basic language, word repetition, and whimsical illustrations, ideal for sharing with your emergent reader

BEGINNING READING
Short sentences, familiar words, and simple concepts for children eager to read on their own

READING WITH HELP
Engaging stories, longer sentences, and language play for developing readers

READING ALONE
Complex plots, challenging vocabulary, and high-interest topics for the independent reader

I Can Read Books have introduced children to the joy of reading since 1957. Featuring award-winning authors and illustrators and a fabulous cast of beloved characters, I Can Read Books set the standard for beginning readers.

A lifetime of discovery begins with the magical words **"I Can Read!"**

*Visit www.icanread.com for information
on enriching your child's reading experience.*

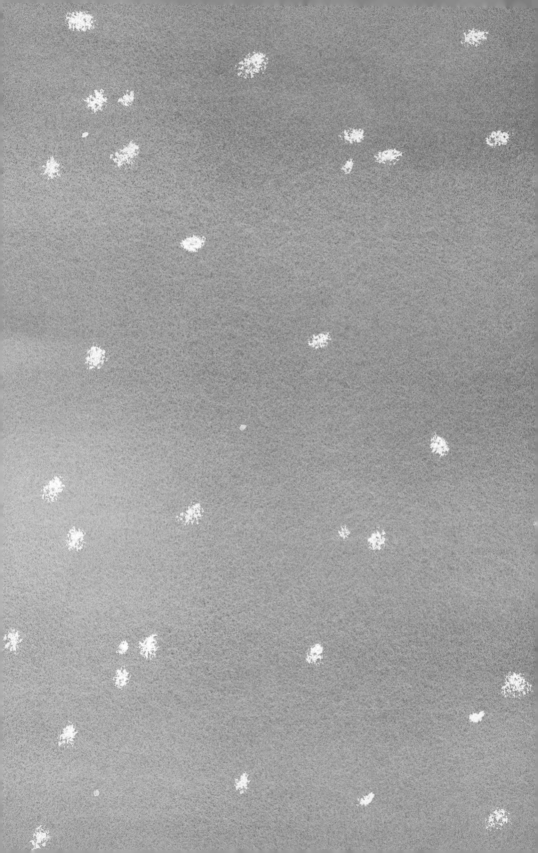

For Pat Schories, with
love and gratitude . . .
—A.S.C.

I Can Read® and I Can Read Book® are trademarks of HarperCollins Publishers.

Biscuit's Snow Day Race. Text copyright © 2019 by Alyssa Satin Capucilli. Illustrations copyright © 2019 by Pat Schories. All rights reserved. Manufactured in the U.S.A. No part of this book may be used or reproduced in any manner whatsoever without written permission except in the case of brief quotations embodied in critical articles and reviews. For information address HarperCollins Children's Books, a division of HarperCollins Publishers, 195 Broadway, New York, NY 10007.
www.icanread.com

Library of Congress Control Number: 2018958433
ISBN 978-0-06-243621-4 (trade bdg.)—ISBN 978-0-06-243620-7 (pbk.)

Typography by Brenda Angelilli

21 22 CWM 10 9 8 7   ❖ First Edition

My First
SHARED READING

I Can Read!

Biscuit's Snow Day Race

story by ALYSSA SATIN CAPUCILLI
pictures by PAT SCHORIES

HARPER
An Imprint of HarperCollinsPublishers

Look, Biscuit.

It's snowing!

Woof, woof!

It's a great day to build
a snow fort, Biscuit.
Woof, woof!

We have our shovel.

Woof!

And you know just how to dig!

Woof, woof!

Are you ready to help,
Biscuit?
Woof!

Oh, Biscuit.

You found a sled.

Woof, woof!

But no sledding yet.
We need to build
our snow fort.

13

This way, Biscuit.
It takes a lot of digging
to build a snow fort.

Are you ready to help?
Woof, woof!

Funny puppy.

What are you up to now?

Woof!

Not the sled again!
Woof, woof!

Come along, now.
We have to build
our snow fort.

Look, Biscuit!

A race is about to begin.

Woof!

Stop, Biscuit.
Come back!

Woof, woof!

Silly puppy.

That's not your sled!

Woof!

Biscuit, hold on!

Woof, woof, woof, woof!

Oh, Biscuit.

You won the race!

Woof, woof!

You had lots
of snowy day fun, too.
Woof!

This way now, Biscuit.
Our snow fort is all set
at last.

There's room for everyone.

Woof, woof!

And snow day treats
for all!
Woof, woof!

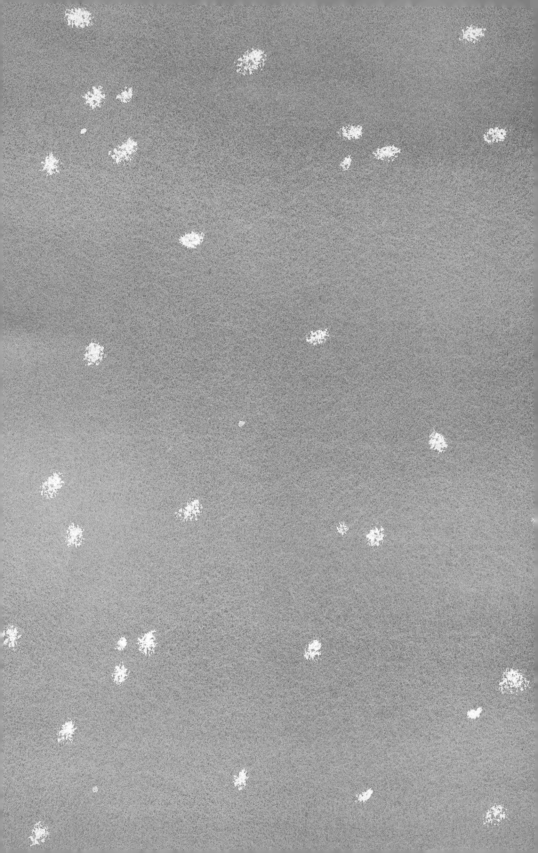

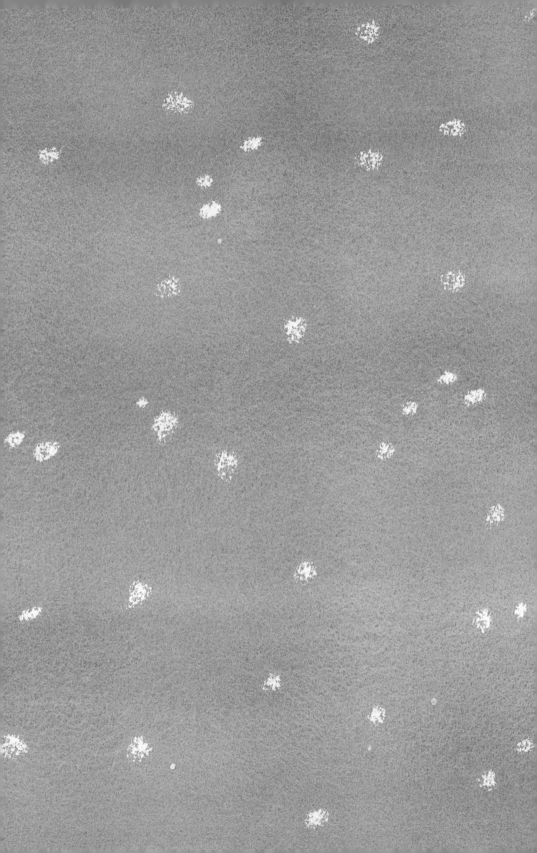